EASTER EGG HUNT!

Once you shop...You can't stop!

SIZZLE PRESS

It was Easter in Shopville and Cheeky Chocolate was planning a special egg hunt. The Shopkins all cheered with delight when they saw her carrying a box full of pretty Easter eggs.

"I'm sure I hid an egg behind that log,"
said Cheeky Chocolate to Eggchic.
"Yes, you did," said Eggchic, "but I collected
all the eggs myself earlier."
"Why would you do that?" asked Cheeky Chocolate.

"I'm sorry," said Eggchic. "I wanted to surprise everyone with a special Easter egg hunt, including you! I hid the Easter eggs in Shopville. . . come and see!" Everyone followed Eggchic back to Shopville.

"I've found the first egg!" cried Dusty Cocoa, jumping up and down with joy.

"And here's another," said Candy Bowl. She was pleased her egg had pretty pink wrapping.

The Shopkins excitedly ran around Shopville, searching for eggs.
"Look!" shouted Shelly Egg as she spotted an Easter egg behind a stool in the boutique.

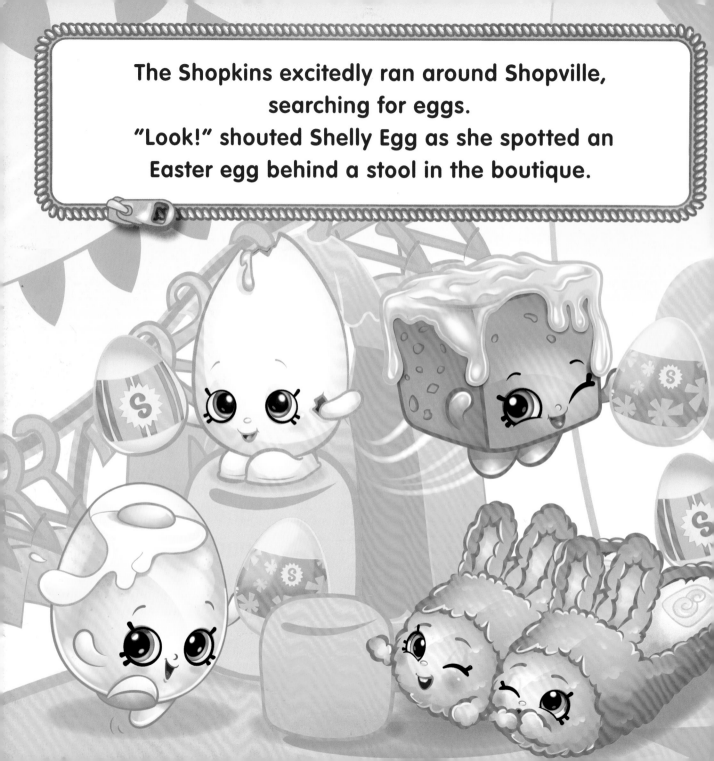

Kay Cupcake showed off her Easter egg, too. She couldn't wait to eat it! Soon, there were delighted shrieks ringing through Shopville as more and more Shopkins found the eggs.

Choc N' Chip were desperate to find an egg each.
And they did! They found two eggs under a table in
the bakery! Eggchic looked on, feeling very happy that
everyone was enjoying her egg hunt.

"Mmm! Delicious!" cried Choc N' Chip. Their eggs didn't last long!

"This is the best Easter egg hunt ever!" said a very happy Harvey Honeycomb.

The only one who hadn't found an egg yet was Cheeky Chocolate. "Don't worry, I'll help you!" said Eggchic. Suddenly, Cheeky Chocolate ran toward a basket. And there, under all the fruit, was the last egg.

Everyone cheered. Cheeky Chocolate looked at Eggchic and smiled. "Clever Eggchic," she said. "Shopville is the perfect place to have an Easter egg hunt!" All the Shopkins agreed.

HAPPY EASTER!

"Can I help you hide them?" Eggchic whispered to Cheeky Chocolate. "I'm really good at hiding things." "No," said Cheeky Chocolate, kindly. "It will spoil the hunt if you know where the eggs are hidden!"

Eggchic secretly followed Cheeky Chocolate to the field. She hid behind a bush, watching as Cheeky Chocolate hid the eggs in bushes, under trees, and in long tufts of grass.

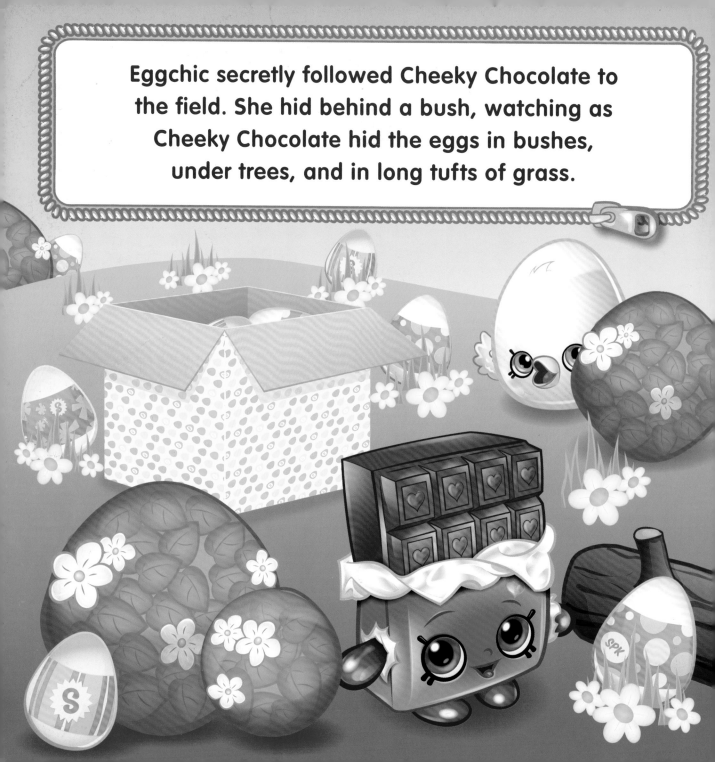

Ready! thought Cheeky Chocolate as she headed back to Shopville.

An Easter egg hunt throughout Shopville would be much more exciting, thought Eggchic. I'll collect the eggs and hide them there instead!

Eggchic tried hard to remember where each egg was hidden. She ran around, quickly searching every bush and tuft of grass. *I must hurry*, she thought, picking up an egg hidden behind a log.

Soon, Eggchic had found every egg. She put them all in the box that Cheeky Chocolate had left behind and raced back to Shopville. She already had clever hiding places in mind.

Eggchic could hear the other Shopkins setting off to the field to hunt for eggs. They were bursting with excitement. Eggchic was excited, too. She was going to give them a fantastic egg hunt right here in Shopville!

"I can't wait," said Kay Cupcake. "I bet I can find the most Easter eggs. No one's better at finding things than me!"

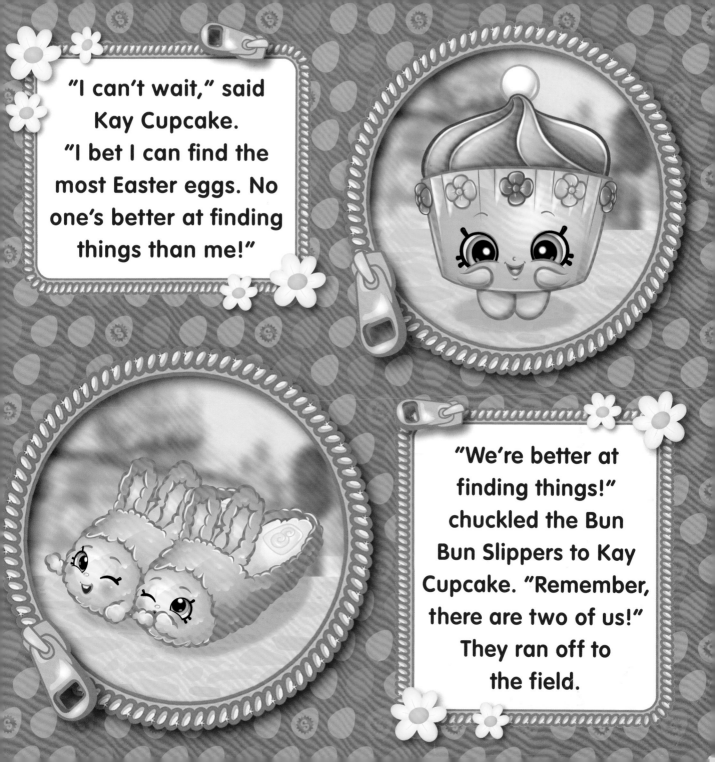

"We're better at finding things!" chuckled the Bun Bun Slippers to Kay Cupcake. "Remember, there are two of us!" They ran off to the field.

Eggchic ran around Shopville, hiding all the eggs. She wanted to give her friends a real challenge to make the hunt extra *egg*-citing. She went to all the shops in Shopville and hid the eggs in the best hiding places.

Eggchic chuckled to herself. Her friends were going to have so much fun! Soon, she only had a couple of eggs left in the box. She thought hard about where to hide them.

Eggchic thought the burger bar was a fun place to hide the eggs. She hoped her friends would think so, too. She looked out of the window and saw the last of the Shopkins heading to the field.

"Hurry up," said Googy to Choc N' Chip. "We are going to miss the Easter egg hunt!"

"Race you!" cried Choc N' Chip. They all ran as fast as they could.

Eggchic followed everyone to the field. When she arrived, she noticed her friends looked disappointed. They were searching hard, but they couldn't find any Easter eggs. Cheeky Chocolate was puzzled.